O'BRIEN panda legends

PANDA books are for young readers
making their own way
through books.

O'BRIEN SERIES FOR YOUNG READERS

O'BRIEN panda cubs

O'BRIEN pandas

O'BRIEN panda legends

O'BRIEN flyers

Can YOU spot the sword

hidden in the story?

The Baby Giant

Words and pictures
• Oisín McGann •

THE O'BRIEN PRESS
DUBLIN

For Milo

First published 2009 by The O'Brien Press Ltd,
12 Terenure Road East, Rathgar, Dublin 6, Ireland.
Tel: +353 1 4923333; Fax: +353 1 4922777
E-mail: books@obrien.ie; Website: www.obrien.ie

Copyright for text © Oisín McGann 2009
Copyright for illustrations, layout, editing and design
© The O'Brien Press Ltd

ISBN: 978-1-84717-088-0

British Library Cataloguing-in-Publication Data
McGann, Oisin
The baby giant. - (Panda Legends series)
1. Children's stories
I. Title
823.9'2[J]

The O'Brien Press receives assistance from

1 2 3 4 5 6 7 8 9 10
09 10 11 12 13 14 15

Typesetting, layout, editing, design: The O'Brien Press Ltd
Printed and bound in the UK by CPI Group

A story of old times
and new –
a story of all times.

Many years ago,
there was a giant called
Finn MacCool.

He was happy –
and hairy –
and was the
biggest, **strongest**
giant in Ireland.

Finn spent most of his time
fighting bullies.

But he was a friendly man.
He was tired of fighting.

One day, he said to his wife,
'I need a holiday.'

'Great!' she said.
'I'd love to go to **Scotland**.
But, you know,
I don't like going on boats.'

His wife's name was Úna.
She wasn't scared of much,
but she was scared of the sea.

'Don't you worry,'
Finn told her.
'I'll build a **bridge** for you.'

So Finn went down
to the seaside.
He started digging **rocks**
out of the cliffs
and jamming them
into the ground
in front of him.

Soon, they reached
far out into the sea
like a bridge.

Finn worked for a week.
He built a bridge of stones
all the way to Scotland.
Then he walked
all the way
back to Ireland
across his bridge.

When he got home,
Finn was very, very tired.

He put on his pyjamas
and went straight to bed.

'I'm going to sleep, Úna!'
he called to his wife.
'I'm all worn out!'

'Grand, so!' said Úna.
'We can go
to Scotland tomorrow,
when you're feeling better.'

'I'll make some sandwiches
and we can have a picnic
on the new bridge
on our way to Scotland.
You have a nice sleep, now,
and I'll wake you up
in the morning.'

Úna stayed up late,
making a huge mountain
of sandwiches.

As she was going to bed,
Úna heard a
booming sound
coming from
far across the sea.

Boom! Boom! Boom!

She thought it was just
the noise of the waves.
She shook her head
and went upstairs.

'Terrible storm out there!'
she said to Finn.
But Finn was snoring away
and didn't even hear her.

The next morning,
the sound was louder.
Boom! Boom! Boom!

Boom! Boom! Boom! Boom!

Finn was still fast asleep,
so Úna went up to
the top of the cliffs
on her own.

She looked out over the sea.
Far out on the stone bridge,
Úna saw a **gigantic man**
walking towards Ireland.

The booming was
the sound of his feet
hitting the stones.

BOOM! BOOM! BOOM!

Úna rushed back to the house
and into the bedroom.

'Finn, wake up!'
she cried.

She shook his shoulder.

'There's a great big giant
coming from Scotland!
He's even bigger and hairier
than you are!'

Finn woke up
very quickly!
'I know him,' he said.
'He's a **bully**.'

'And he's as big
as two normal giants,'
Finn said.
'He's nasty and mean
and he won't **play fair**.
All Scotland is scared of him.
He'll want to fight me,
but I'm too tired for a fight.
He'll beat me up for sure.'

'Don't you worry,'
Úna said to him.
'We'll think of something.'

They thought hard
for a while
and at last
they came up
with a **plan**.

'We'll have to be quick,'
said Finn.

'I'll go and make
the special buns,'
Úna told him.
'You make the baby's cot.'

The booming got louder.
The Scottish Giant's feet
crunched down
on the Irish seaside.
The ground shook.

BOOM!

BOOM!

BOOM!

BOOM!

'**WHERE** IS
FINN MacCOOL?'

a voice roared.

'I WANT A FIGHT
AND I WANT IT **NOW!**
I'M **NASTY** AND MEAN
AND I **WON'T**
PLAY FAIR!'

'COME OUT,

FINN MacCOOL,'

he roared,

'IF YOU'RE BRAVE

ENOUGH!'

Finn did not answer.
He was too busy making
a big, wooden baby's **cot**.

Úna did not answer.

She was too busy knitting.

She was making

a huge **bonnet**

and a pair of **pyjamas**

with pictures of

teddy bears on them.

Her **special buns** were

baking in the oven.

Their house began to shake
as the Scottish Giant
walked towards it.

Úna finished the
pyjamas and bonnet
and Finn quickly put them on.

Now he looked like
a **huge baby**.

He stuck a **big soother**
in his mouth and
climbed into the cot.
He pulled a blanket
over himself
and lay still.

The Scottish Giant
smashed open the door
and walked in.

He had arms like **tree-trunks**
and legs like **lamp-posts**
and he had a face
like a **bulldog**.

'WHERE IS

FINN MacCOOL?'

he shouted.

'Oh, he's out
catching **sharks**
with his **teeth**,'
Úna replied.
'He'll be back
in a few minutes.
Would you like a bun
while you wait?'

The Scottish Giant
grunted
and then nodded.

Úna opened the oven
and took out the tray of buns.

But these were not
normal buns.
Úna had put **stones**
in some of them.
She gave a bun to the giant.
(It had stones in it.)

She gave a bun to Finn
who was still hidden
under the blanket.
(Finn's bun had no stones in it.)

Finn took out his soother
and popped the bun
into his mouth.
He ate it in one big bite.

But when the giant
bit into his bun,
it **broke his tooth**.

'Ouch! Ooh! Eeeh!'
screamed the Scottish Giant.
'These are hard buns!'

'Are they?' Úna said.
'Well, the **baby** loves them.'

She gave Finn another bun.

(Finn's bun had no stones in it.)

He chomped it down easily.

Úna gave the giant
a second bun.

(This one had stones in it too.)

'Ouch!' the giant said,
as he broke some more teeth.
'What kind of a **child** eats
buns like these?'

The giant stood up.
He stomped over to the cot
to get a **closer look**
at this baby.
He leaned over
the side of the cot
and stared down
at the big body
under the blanket.

'How can this be
Finn MacCool's **baby**?'
he asked.
'Look how **big** he is!'

'Yes! And he's only
two years old,'
Úna told him.
'Isn't he lovely?'

'**Ga-ga**,' said Finn.
The giant pulled back the
blanket and stared.

He plucked the soother
out of Finn's mouth.
'*Ga-ga*!' Finn growled.

He jumped up.
He was still dressed
in his teddy-bear pyjamas
and his big bonnet.

He opened his mouth wide
and **bit** the giant
on the hand.

'AAAH!'

screamed the giant.
'That baby nearly
bit my hand off!'

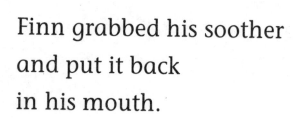

Finn grabbed his soother
and put it back
in his mouth.

'But he's only being friendly,'
said Úna with a smile.
'He's just excited.
He knows his daddy
will be home soon.'

'**Da-da**!' said Finn.

The giant stared
at the huge thing in the cot.
If this was Finn MacCool's
baby, what kind of **monster**
was Finn MacCool?

The Scottish Giant
did **not** want to find out.

He turned
and ran for the door.
He ran down to the seaside
and across the stone bridge.
Then he ran all the way
back to Scotland.

He even **smashed up**
the bridge behind him
so that Finn
could not follow him.

But Finn did not want
to follow him.
Finn and Úna
decided to stay at home
for their holidays.

They had a picnic
down at the seaside
and drank apple juice
and ate buns ...

with no stones in them.